Kids, meet the King of the Jungle!

But do Lions live
in the jungle?
No. They live
in grasslands
and plains.

Lions aren't as friendly as our pet cats and dogs. But what else should we know about them? How do they behave? Are they fast runners? Let's explore cool facts about the lions.

Behind tigers, lions are second in terms of size. Yes, they are the second largest cat species existing today. Male lions could weigh 400 pounds while the females may weigh up to 290 pounds. The heaviest lion ever recorded weighed 826 pounds. This is incredible.

Lions can run up to 50mph. But they can only run fast over a short distance because they lack stamina. They can leap up to 35 feet.

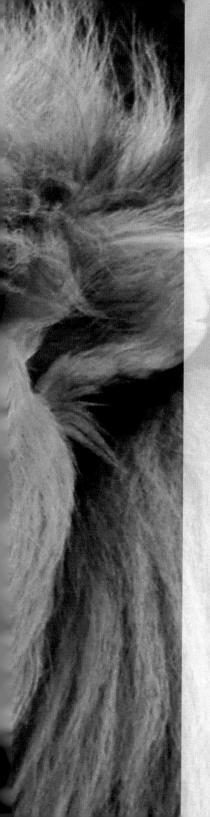

Lions roar. Have you heard their roar? Maybe in the movies. Their roar can be heard even though you're 8 kilometers away from them. That's extremely loud.

Lions in the wild are found in southern and eastern Africa.

Lions live in groups called "prides" with females, their young and few adult males. They are considered as highly sociable animals. The pride is composed of about 15 lions.

How can we identify the male lions from the females? Male lions are easy to identify because of their manes. Lionesses or female lions are often attracted to male lions with darker manes.

Which do you think are good hunters? Is it the males or the lioness?

Well, the females or the lionesses are the good hunters. They usually go out to hunt for food for their pride.

What about the males? What is their main responsibility? The male lion protects and defends the pride's territory.

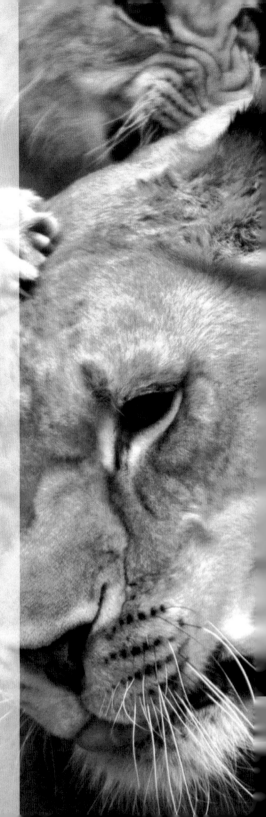

Even though the females do the hunting, the male lions will eat first. That's quite unfair. But that is how it has always been.

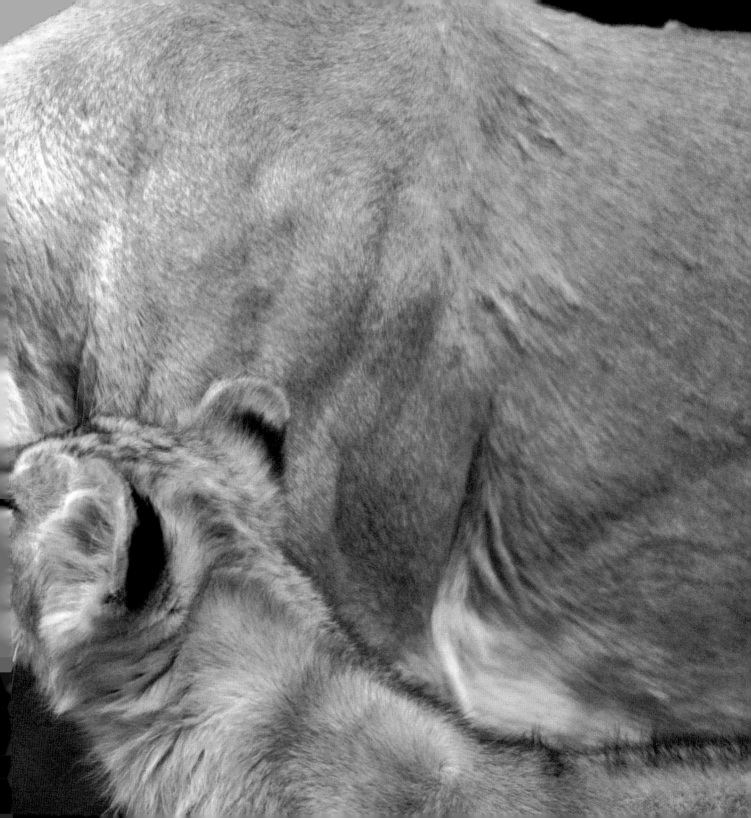

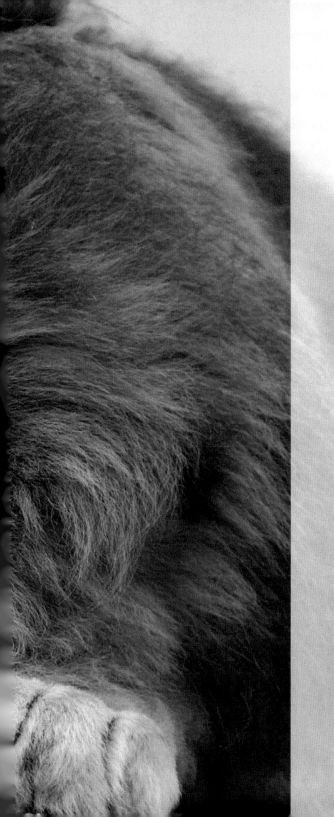

Lions love to take a rest. They may use as much as 20 hours a day to rest.

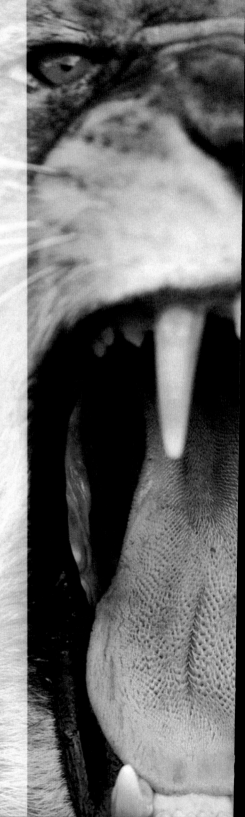

These great cats have their heels lifted when they walk. Yes, their heels don't touch the ground when they walk. Let's try to imagine how they do it.

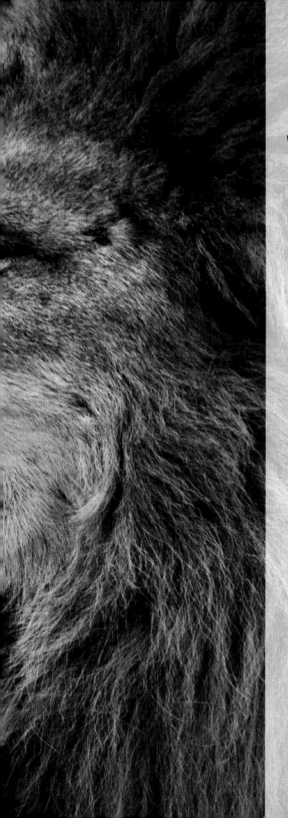

What if a lion and a tiger meet? Will they be attracted to each other and breed? Yes, that's possible. The hybrids are called ligers and tigons.

Lions are the national animal of countries like Singapore, Belgium, the Netherlands, and the ancient kingdom of Alania, which is now in Iran.

Being one of the most threatened animals in the world, we have to protect these majestic cats so they don't leave us forever. Lions are ferocious beasts. They symbolize power.

Lions radiate strength and ferocity. How would you feel if you happened to see a lion up close? Would it be an amazing or frightening experience?

Made in the USA
Monee, IL
02 December 2020

50440789R00026